HAVE YOU SEEN
THE
DUBLIN VAMPIRE?
ÚNA WOODS

THE O'BRIEN PRESS
DUBLIN

D1294759

In an old part of Dublin, right down by the sea,

There's a moon-shaped park with a creepy old tree.

4

he Dublin Vampire lives there.

The Vampire wakes up as the sun's going down.

He hops on the ghost bus and rides into town.

Have you seen the Dublin Vampire?

As he crosses the Liffey the wind and rain whirl,

And we hurry about in our own little worlds.

Have you seen the Dublin Vampire?

the book
of kells

In the dusty old library in Trinity College

He reads ancient books, full of wisdom and knowledge.

Have you seen the Dublin Vampire?

On Grafton Street, shoppers and buskers and crowds,
All hustle and bustle, and busy and loud!

Have you seen the Dublin Vampire?

In the Dead Zoo he hangs out with badgers and hares,
A spotty giraffe and a huge polar bear.

Have you seen the Dublin Vampire?

In the Green, he says 'hi' to the ducks and the swans
As they fluff up their feathers and splash in the pond.

Have you seen the Dublin Vampire?

In a café he stops for a sweet cherry bun

And a hot drop of tea at a table for one.

Have you seen the Dublin Vampire?

The Castle is lovely at this spooky hour

As his old friend the ghost waves hello from the tower.

Have you seen the Dublin Vampire?

He loves Halloween when folks dress up like him

And fireworks explode with a boom! snap! fizz! zim!

Have you seen the Dublin Vampire?

He watches the people in Temple Bar Square
Who don't even notice that he's also there.

24

Have you seen the Dublin Vampire?

At sunrise the Vampire heads back to his home,

But everyone's busy with traffic and phones.

Have you seen the Dublin Vampire?

So the next time you walk through the city at night,

When Dublin is twinkling in silver moonlight,

You might see the Dublin Vampire.

To Rosie and Dylan

Úna Woods is an illustrator and author who lives in Dublin. She loves making illustrations for children and her work has been published in books, magazines and websites.

She loves working with bright colours and patterns in her illustrations. She grew up in Clontarf, very close to where Bram Stoker was born.
www.unawoods.com

First published 2020 by The O'Brien Press Ltd,
12 Terenure Road East, Rathgar, Dublin 6, D06 HD27, Ireland
Tel: +353 1 4923333; Fax: +353 1 4922777
E-mail: books@obrien.ie
Website: www.obrien.ie
The O'Brien Press is a member of Publishing Ireland.
Reprinted 2020

Published in

DUBLIN
UNESCO
City of Literature

Copyright for text & illustration © Una Woods
Copyright for layout, editing and design
© The O'Brien Press Ltd

ISBN: 978-1-78849-119-8
All rights reserved. No part of this book may be
reproduced or utilised in any way or by any means, electronic
or mechanical, including photocopying, recording or by any
information storage and retrieval system without
permission in writing from the publisher.

6 5 4 3 2
22 21 20

Printed and bound in Poland by Białostockie Zakłady Graficzne S.A.
The paper in this book is produced using pulp from managed forests.

Have You Seen The Dublin Vampire? receives financial assistance from the Arts Council